COMICS

ISSUE #1

XENODOROID

"AWAKENING"

Created By
DEION TILLETT

To order additional copies of this book, contact:
Xlibris
844-714-8691
www.Xlibris.com
Orders@Xlibris.com

ISBN: Softcover   978-1-6698-1952-3
        EBook   978-1-6698-1951-6

Print information available on the last page

Rev. date: 04/05/2022

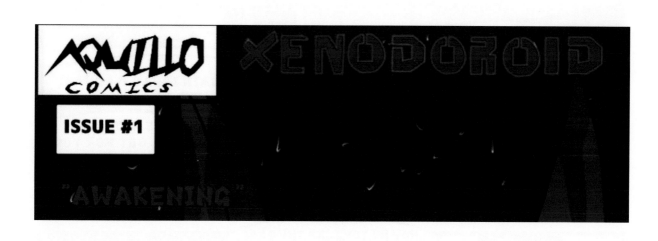

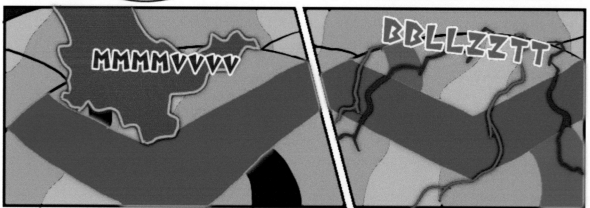

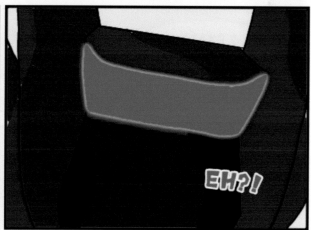

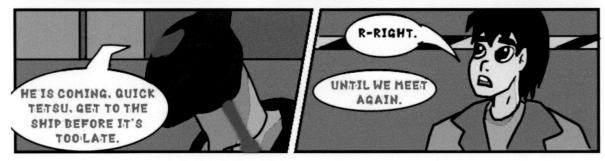

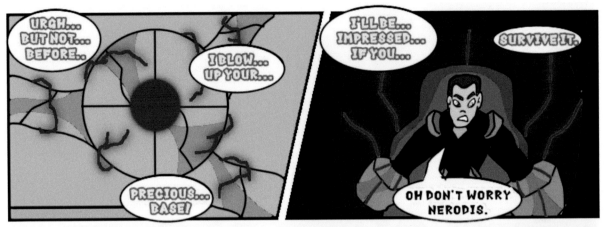

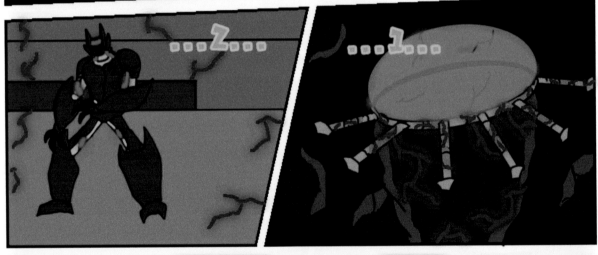

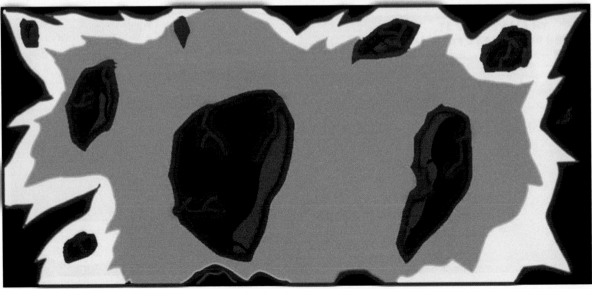

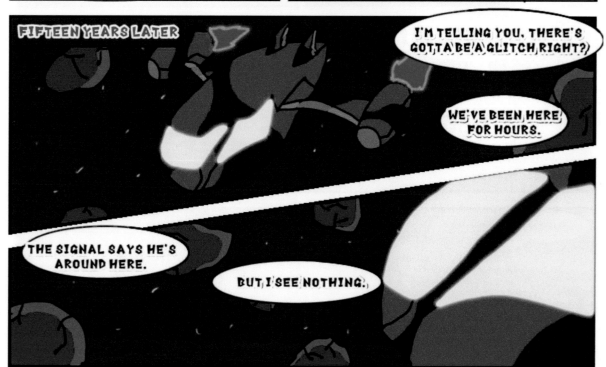

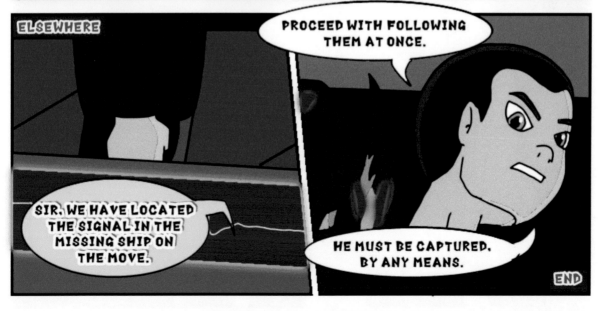

END